St. Malachi's Total Abstinence Relief Society

Constitution, by-laws and rules of St. Malachi's Total Abstinence Relief Society: organized December 20th, 1868, revised December 11th, 1877

Antigonos

St. Malachi's Total Abstinence Relief Society

Constitution, by-laws and rules of St. Malachi's Total Abstinence Relief Society: organized December 20th, 1868, revised December 11th, 1877

Reprint of the original, first published in 1877.

1st Edition 2024 | ISBN: 978-3-38612-111-8

Antigonos Verlag is an imprint of Outlook Verlagsgesellschaft mbH.

Verlag (Publisher): Outlook Verlag GmbH, Zeilweg 44, 60439 Frankfurt, Deutschland, info@outlook-verlag.de
Vertretungsberechtigt (Authorized to represent): E. Roepke, Zeilweg 44, 60439 Frankfurt, Deutschland
Druck (Print): Libri Plureos GmbH, Friedensallee 273, 22763 Hamburg, Deutschland

CONSTITUTION

BY-LAWS AND RULES

OF

ST. MALACHI'S

Total Abstinence Relief Society.

ORGANIZED DECEMBER 20th, 1868.

Revised December 11th, 1877.

ST. JOHN, N. B.:

PRINTED AT THE HERALD OFFICE, GERMAIN STREET.

1877.

APPROVED,

    †J. SWEENY, *Bishop of St. John.*

EPISCOPAL PALACE,
 December 11th, 1877.

CONSTITUTION.

ARTICLE I.—NAME.

This Organization shall be known as the SAINT MALACHI'S TOTAL ABSTINENCE RELIEF SOCIETY.

ARTICLE II.—OBJECT.

Its object shall be the general adoption and encouragement of the principles and practice of Total Abstinence.

ARTICLE III.—MEMBERSHIP.

Sec. 1. No person belonging to any other Temperance organization can become a member of this Society.

Sec. 2. Any person selling intoxicating liquors on his own account, shall not be eligible as a member of this Society.

Sec. 3. Any person who is not of the Catholic religion, of good moral standing, free from disease, and willing to abide by the Constitution and By-Laws, cannot become a member of this Society.

Sec. 4. The Board of Officers reserve to themselves the right of decision on the foregoing points.

ARTICLE IV.—OFFICERS.

The officers of this Society shall be a Spiritual Director, President, Senior and Junior Vice-Presidents, Recording Secretary, Assistant Recording Secretary, Financial Secretary, Assistant Financial Secretary, Treasurer, Sergeant-at-Arms, and a Committee of two members for each Ward of the City (east side,) and two for the Special Ward.

ARTICLE V.—ELECTION OF OFFICERS.

Sec. 1. The Spiritual Director shall be a clergyman appointed by the Bishop of this Diocese. The other officers shall be elected by the members at the Annual Meetings. All elections shall be by ballot.

Sec. 2. Should any office become vacant before the expiration of the term, a member shall be elected thereto, at the next regular meeting.

Sec. 3. No member shall be eligible for office unless he have been at least six months in the Society, and have paid all his dues up to period of election.

ARTICLE VI.—Duties of Officers.

Sec. 1. The Spiritual Director shall administer the Total Abstinence Pledge to each member on his initiation; and shall be consulted on all matters of importance.

Sec. 2. The President shall preside at the meetings; shall preserve order thereat; shall decide all points of order (subject to appeal to the Society), and shall maintain the observance of the rules.

Sec. 3. When the President is absent, the next senior officer shall occupy the chair and perform his duties.

Sec. 4. It shall be the duty of the Recording Secretary to keep a correct record of all business of the Society, and keep a correct roll of all members of the Society, in a book to be kept for that purpose, with the dates of their admission, resignation, or otherwise; call roll of officers and committees; read Minutes of preceding meeting, and submit, at each annual meeting, a written statement recapitulating the business done by the Society during the year then ending, and showing its relative standing; and give such other information as may be required by the Society; in his absence the Assistant Recording Secretary shall perform his duties.

Sec. 5.   It shall be the duty of the Financial Secretary to keep the account of each member of the Society, to receive all initiation fees, dues and fines, and pay the same over to the Treasurer at each meeting, he taking a receipt for the same, in a book to be kept for that purpose, and to report quarterly at the semi-monthly meetings of March, June, September and December, of all moneys received by him for such periods, and of the indebtedness of each member of the Society; in his absence, the Assistant Financial Secretary shall perform his duties.

Sec. 6.   It shall be the duty of the Treasurer to receive all moneys from the Financial Secretary, and pay all bills ordered by the Society and none others, and shall take a receipt for the same; he shall report the amounts by him received and disbursed at the semi-monthly meetings of March, June, September and December; he shall also give up all money, papers, &c., in his hands when requested by the Society, and also give a receipt to the Financial Secretary at each meeting of the Society for all money by him received.

Sec. 7. The duty of the Sergeant-at-Arms shall be to see that none are present but members, or persons intending to become members, on any evening of meetings, except by leave of the President, or in his absence the next senior officer, and carry out the instructions of the President, or in his absence the next senior officer, in preserving order.

Sec. 8. The Ward Committees shall, upon being notified, visit forthwith any sick member residing in their district, and if, in their judgment, he be entitled to relief, give an order on the Treasurer for the same, and report the case at the next regular meeting, after which the sanction of the Society shall be required for its continuance. The sick shall be visited by their respective Committees at least once a week.

ARTICLE VII.—Quorum.

Fifteen members shall constitute a quorum for the transaction of business concerning the Society.

ARTICLE VIII.—Processions.

When a procession is to be ordered the President, or in his absence his representative, shall appoint to the charge any member, who in turn may choose his assistants from the members of the Society.

ARTICLE IX.—The Pledge.

Sec. 1. Every member, on his initiation, shall take the following pledge before the Spiritual Director, or any other clergyman, (or produce a certificate showing that he has already done so) in the sense of the annexed conditions :

"I promise, with the Divine assistance and in honor of the sacred thirst of our Saviour on the cross, to abstain from the use of all intoxicating drinks; and to discountenance the cause and practice of intemperance."

Sec. 2. By taking the Pledge a member shall therefore be held himself not only to abstain, but in no way to co-operate in the practice of intemperance, or encourage it in others.

Sec. 3. The duration of the Pledge shall be as long as the Society lasts.

Sec. 4. Intoxicating liquors used as medicine, and prescribed as such by a conscientious physician, are not included in this Pledge.

ARTICLE X.—AMENDMENTS, &c.

Alterations, amendments, or additions to this Constitution, may be made by a two-thirds vote of the members present at any meeting of the Society.

BY-LAWS.

ARTICLE I.—Meetings.

Sec. 1. Annual meetings for the election of Officers shall be held on the last Sunday of December each year.

Sec. 2. Regular meetings shall be held on the second and last Sundays of each month.

Sec. 3. Special meetings may be called at any time by the sanction of the President.

Sec. 4. Due notice of each meeting shall be given through the public press.

Sec. 5. The place of meeting shall be St. Malachi's Hall; the hour half-past seven o'clock, p. m.

Sec. 6. No meeting shall be prolonged beyond ten o'clock, p. m., unless by a majority vote of members present.

ARTICLE II.—Fees and Dues.

Sec. 1. Every member on his enrolment shall pay an initiation fee of twenty-five cents.

Sec. 2. Every member shall pay into the funds the sum of Twenty cents monthly.

Sec. 3. The dues of sick members (unless otherwise paid) shall be deducted from their relief allowance.

ARTICLE III.—Benefits.

Sec. 1. A Low Mass will be offered by the Spiritual Director every Saturday for the benefit of the living and dead members of the Society.

Sec. 2. A Low Mass will be offered for every deceased actual member within the week following his death.

Sec. 3. All members when sick shall be entitled to the sum of Two Dollars per week, not exceeding eight weeks in any twelve months.

Sec. 4. On the decease of any actual member the Society shall expend, as relief, in money ·or otherwise, as it may deem proper, the sum of Twenty Dollars, to defray funeral expenses.

Sec. 5. On the decease of any actual member the Recording Secretary shall, upon being notified, give notice through the public press ·of the time and place of the funeral; and the members will be expected to attend the same.

Sec. 6. No person shall be entitled to benefits unless he have been a regular member for at least six successive months, and have paid his dues in full for that period.

Sec. 7. Any member whose dues are three months in arrears, cannot claim any of the benefits of actual members, unless such member be sick, (when he shall be dealt with as already provided,) or absent from the city.

Sec. 8. Orders for relief shall be discontinued whenever the funds are insufficient to meet such demands.

ARTICLE IV.—Fines.

Sec. 1. All Officers and Committees absent from regularly called meetings shall be fined Twenty-five cents, unless they show a good and reasonable cause for such absence.

Sec. 2. Any member who, during the transaction of business, leaves the meeting without the permission of the Chairman, shall be fined Ten cents.

ARTICLE V.—Miscellaneous.

Sec. 1. Any member refusing to abide by the Constitution, By-Laws, or Rules, or guilty of any misdemeanor calculated to discredit the Society, shall, upon proof thereof, be subject to censure, or expulsion, as a majority of the members present, at any regular meeting, may determine.

Sec. 2. All members expelled the Society shall, upon re-admission, be subject to the rules for the initiation of members.

Sec. 3. All members expelled, when indebted to the Society, shall, when re-admitted, be held responsible for the amount due at the date of expulsion.

Sec. 4. The Ward Committees shall, each in turn, as called by the Secretary, collect at the doors on public lecture nights ; and the others shall preserve order in the hall.

Sec. 5. On the Second Sunday of each month a Public Lecture will be delivered under the auspices and for the benefit of the Society. Such lectures to be attended by all members wearing their badges.

Sec. 6. Business done on Lecture nights shall be confined to administering the pledge, initiation of, and receiving the dues from members and the reception of reports from committees.

Sec. 7. All members are requested to attend

the public meetings and encourage, by all possible means, the principles and practice of Total Abstinence.

Sec. 8. All bills shall be paid out of the funds of the Society.

Sec. 9. The Treasurer is the only person who can pay any bill, and he shall require the sanction of this Society for all bills so paid, unless it be an order for relief.

Sec. 10. No dues shall be refunded to any person leaving the Society, let the cause be what it will.

Sec. 11. All members nominated for any office shall be elected by ballot, unless there is no opposition.

Sec. 12. Every member, on paying his initiation fee, will receive a Register Ticket, which he will present at the regular meetings to have registered thereon, by the Financial Secretary, his payments of monthly dues.

Sec. 13. On the decease of any member, the Committee of the Ward in which he resided shall, if necessary, ascertain from the Financial Secretary whether he was in good standing on the books, and, if such be the case, to report the same to the Recording Secretary.

Sec. 14. All the members shall go to Confession and Communion at least twice a year.

Sec. 15. The Recording Secretary shall audit all accounts of the Society.

Sec. 16. A Gas Committee of two members shall be appointed each year at the annual election.

Sec. 17. In the event of the Society's meetings being suspended, the President, or in his absence the next senior officer, is hereby held—six months after the last regular meeting—to call a meeting of all the members, not in arrears at the time of suspension, for the purpose of voting and delivering to some charitable Institution or Society, under the patronage of the Bishop, all moneys remaining in the hands of the Treasurer, after the payment of all bills and expenses contracted thereto by the Society.

Sec. 18. The Society shall have, according to their discretion, the right to deal with all cases and circumstances not herein provided for.

RULES OF ORDER.

---

1. The Chairman shall not make or second any motion, nor shall he vote on any question except in case of a tie.

2. When a member speaks or offers a motion, he shall rise in his place and respectfully address the Chair.

3. When two or more members rise at the same time, the Chairman shall decide who has the floor.

4. When a member is called to order, he shall take his seat until the point is decided.

5. A motion shall be seconded, and afterwards repeated from the Chair, before it is debated.

6. A member who shall have made a motion may, by consent of the seconder, withdraw or alter it before it is discussed; but the consent of the meeting shall be necessary if the debate has commenced.

7. When a question is under debate, the only motions in order shall be: 1st, to amend; 2nd, to amend an amendment; 3rd, to adjourn; 4th, to lie on the table; 5th, the previous question; 6th, to postpone; 7th, to refer to a committee; 8th, to divide.

8. It shall be at the discretion of the Chairman to put or not a motion when an amendment of the nature of a full and distinct proposition is carried; and the same principle shall be applied when an amendment to an amendment of the same nature is carried.

9. Motion of adjournment shall take precedence of all other business, and shall be put to the meeting without debate or amendment.

1ɔ. When the previous question is moved and seconded, it shall be put in this form, "Shall the main question be now put?" If this is carried, all further debate or amendments shall be precluded, and the question put without delay, commencing with the amendments (if any) first, and concluding with the original motion.

11. A motion of reconsideration shall not be in order, unless made by a member who had previously voted with the majority.

12. When the Chairman's decision of the result of a vote is questioned, the Recording Secretary shall count the votes and report to the Chair the number of affirmative and negative votes.

13. A motion affecting the funds to the extent of Twenty Dollars or more, shall not be in order unless notice of such motion be given at a preceding meeting.

14. No member shall be allowed to speak more than twice and not longer than five minutes at a time upon any subject, unless by leave of the Chairman.

ORDER OF BUSINESS.

1. Lecture.
2. Initiation of Members.
3. Roll Call of Officers and Committees.
4. Roll Call of Members, Quarterly.
5. Reading of Minutes.
6. Payment of Dues.
7. Report of Standing Committees.
8. Quarterly Official Reports.
9. Annual Report of Secretary.
10. Reports of Special Committees.
11. Bills against the Society presented.
12. Adjourned Business.
13. Election of Officers and Committees.
14. Miscellaneous business.
15. Receipts of the Evening.
16. Adjournment.